For the children of Chapelton Avenue – JD

For Rory and Hamish – LM

First published 2011 by Macmillan Children's Books
This edition published 2018 by Macmillan Children's Books
an imprint of Pan Macmillan
20 New Wharf Road, London N1 9RR
Associated companies throughout the world
www.panmacmillan.com

ISBN: 978-1-5098-6272-6

1 3 5 7 9 8 6 4 2

A CIP catalogue record for this book is available
from the British Library.

Printed in China.

The Rhyming Rabbit

WRITTEN BY
JULIA DONALDSON

ILLUSTRATED BY
LYDIA MONKS

MACMILLAN CHILDREN'S BOOKS

The Rhyming Rabbit was sitting
with his family in a grassy field.
All the other rabbits were eating
the grass, but the Rhyming Rabbit
was making up a poem about it:

Grass is growing all around.
It makes a lovely swishing sound.
It looks so green, it smells so sweet,
And – best of all – it's good to eat.

"Stop rhyming! Start eating!"
said the other rabbits.

It was beginning to get dark when one of the
rabbits pricked up his ears and stamped a foot.
"Fox!" he shouted.
Straight away, all the rabbits ran to their burrow.
All except for the Rhyming Rabbit, who closed
his eyes and made up a poem
about the fox:

O fearful fox, all rusty red,
You fill our rabbit hearts with dread.
So silently you crouch and sniff
Until you catch our rabbit whiff.
So hungrily, you cunning beast,
You stalk your tasty rabbit feast.
You're sly and crafty, through and through –
But we can run as fast as you!

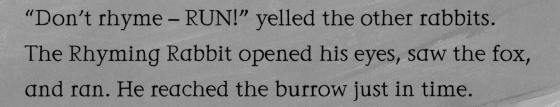

"Don't rhyme – RUN!" yelled the other rabbits.
The Rhyming Rabbit opened his eyes, saw the fox,
and ran. He reached the burrow just in time.

It was night-time. The tired rabbits
lay down together in their burrow.
All except for the Rhyming Rabbit
who sat apart from the others,
singing a song to them:

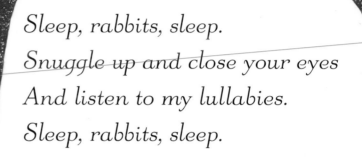

Sleep, rabbits, sleep.
Snuggle up and close your eyes
And listen to my lullabies.
Sleep, rabbits, sleep.

Dream, rabbits, dream,
Of grassy fields and sunny hours
And cabbages and cauliflowers.
Dream, rabbits, dream.

"Stop singing – go to sleep!"
said the other rabbits.

The Rhyming Rabbit felt sad and lonely. The other rabbits were all snoring but he couldn't get to sleep.

The others do nothing but moan. I'm going to go off on my own,

he said to himself, and he started to dig.

He dug a long tunnel, and to keep himself going he made up a short digging poem:

Dig, dig! Quick, quick!
Scrabble, scrabble! Kick, kick!

The tunnel led him up and down
and round a corner, where he met
a worm. The Rhyming Rabbit
stopped in his tracks and made
up a new poem:

Wonderful worm, deep in the soil,
Why do you wiggle and curl and coil?
Where are you going? Where have you been?
How do you manage to stay so clean?
How do you change your shape like that,
From long and skinny to short and fat?
And – one more thing that's been bothering me –
How can you bear to eat earth for tea?

But the worm said nothing.
He had no ears, so he couldn't
hear the poem.

Round the next corner, the Rhyming Rabbit
met a mole. The mole's eyes were very
small but he did have ears.
Maybe he would enjoy a spot of poetry.
The Rhyming Rabbit stood on his
hind legs and began to recite:

Marvellous mole, as black as coal,
With shovelling toes and pointed nose
You snuffle around beneath the ground.
You're practically blind, but never mind;
At least you can hear, so lend an ear
And hear when I say, "Moles rule okay!"

"Be quiet," said the mole.
"I'm looking for worms."

The Rhyming Rabbit felt very lonely, but he carried on digging. He dug and he dug till he met a centipede. Straight away, he thought up his best poem yet:

O centipede with a hundred legs,
Supposing you laid a hundred eggs?
And supposing the baby centipedes had
A hundred legs like their mum and dad,
How many legs would **that** be?

And supposing the baby centipedes grew
And they each laid a hundred eggs like you,
And all of the new little sisters and brothers
Had just the same number of legs as the others,
How many legs would **THAT** be?

"Shut up," said the centipede. "I hate sums."

The Rhyming Rabbit felt sadder and
lonelier than ever. And he felt hungry too.
He dug his way up out of the earth and
into the open air, and found himself on a
hill. The grass was covered in dew. It tasted
delicious. The Rhyming Rabbit ate and ate
till he felt much better. Then he gazed up at
the night sky and made up a new poem:

O midnight-blue and velvet sky!
O silver stars, so bright and high!
O yellow moon, so clear and full,
That shines on trees and grass and . . .
and . . . and . . .

The Rhyming Rabbit couldn't think
of a rhyme for "full".

He stopped and scratched his head.

"Wool!" said a voice. The Rhyming Rabbit turned round
and saw a woolly sheep standing beside him.
"Thank you, Sheep – you found a rhyme!" he said,
and the sheep replied: "I make up poems all the time."

Another poet! The Rhyming Rabbit stared in wonder.
Before he could think of a rhyming reply, the sheep went on:

How nice it is to meet a rabbit
With whom to share my rhyming habit.

The Rhyming Rabbit felt so happy that he
decided to make up a poem for the sheep:

O pretty and poetic sheep
Who stands upon the hill so steep,
With handsome horns and woolly fleece,
As white as snow, or clouds, or . . . or . . . or . . .

"*Geese?*" suggested the sheep.
She smiled at the rabbit and added,
"*Shall I make up a poem for you?*"
"*Oh yes, I pray you, sheep, please do!*"
replied the Rhyming Rabbit.

So the sheep cleared her throat and recited:

Any old rabbit can dig.
Any old rabbit can feed,
But a rabbit who knows how to make up poems
Is a special rabbit indeed.

Any old rabbit can run.
Any old rabbit can sleep,
But only a very special rabbit
Could make up poems with a sheep.

The Rhyming Rabbit sighed happily.

The sun came up. It was a beautiful day. The Rhyming Rabbit and the sheep stayed together all day, making up poems about the sun and the flowers and the trees.

As evening fell and their shadows grew long,
the Rhyming Rabbit remembered his family
back in the burrow, and he said to the sheep,

The others must be getting worried.
Goodbye, dear friend. It's time I hurried.

The sheep looked very sad, and said,

You go? Oh no!
Oh woe! Oh sorrow!

But the Rhyming Rabbit replied,

I will come back again tomorrow!